Zoey Isabella Sweezy Presents...
Behind the Curtain

the Tooth Fairy

A Journalistic Investigation

Written by **STEVEN STACK**
Illustrated by **JAYDEN SHAMBEAU**

Chloe and Zoe

You two are the reason my world is full
of beauty, wonder, and ridiculousness.
Love you both for forever.

Published by Orange Hat Publishing 2023
ISBN: 9781645384700

www.orangehatpublishing.com

My assistant for this investigation is:

~~~~~~~~~~~~~~~~~~~~~~~~~~~~~~~~~~

DAY 1. SATURDAY. 8:34 A.M.

It all started when I, Zoey Isabella Sweezy, woke up and discovered that, yet again, my tooth, which I carefully placed under my pillow last night, had been removed.

And yes, there was a little coinage left behind.

Note: "Coinage" is short for money, even though coinage has more letters and thus is not actually shorter.

Another Note: I will not disclose the amount left behind because that seems rather personal and perhaps against Tooth Fairy edict, which could lead to my no longer receiving said coinage. That, I would be strongly against.

Anyway, though it had happened multiple times before (seven, to be exact), this time, the discovery raised a question for which an answer was required: why does the Tooth Fairy collect the teeth of children and pay for them?

When you think about it, and I have multiple times, it makes little sense. Or none, actually. Collecting teeth and paying for them seems quite the odd career choice. If I was going to continue to partake in this exchange, I needed to find out what the Tooth Fairy's angle was.

To do this, I needed to investigate,

and investigations take planning.

Knowing that coming up with an investigation would be exhausting, I resolved to take a break for the rest of the day.

Time to go outside and try to teach Ralph, my cat, to meow in a

British accent.

DAY 2. SUNDAY. 9:46 A.M.

After a refreshing night's sleep and a massive bowl of Llama Delight cereal, which is not made of llamas (that I'm aware of), it was time to go back to my room to begin planning my investigation.

Following the scientific method, as all adequate investigators do, I needed to come up with possible reasons, or hypotheses, for why the Tooth Fairy would collect teeth.

Note: After a specific incident, which I shall not discuss here, I have been banned from using hammers or nails for any of my projects.

I raided my collection of multicolored poster board paper, which I had requested from my parents for just this purpose, and taped them up on my walls.

Anywho, back to my hypothesizing. After a painstaking 33 1/3 minutes, I produced five reasons.

Reason One:

The most logical and disturbing one. TF eats them because

Well, technically four, but more on that later.

a) TF loves the taste of children's teeth, or

b) TF needs whatever nutrients the teeth offer.

Note: I hope this isn't the reason.

Another Note: From here on out, the Tooth Fairy will simply be known as "TF" because writing "Tooth Fairy" is tiresome, especially when TF works perfectly fine.

Reason Two:

TF has an enormous mouth that holds billions upon billions of teeth but was born without any teeth of their own. Therefore, TF must collect them to finally be able to chew food and brush their teeth, both of which they have always longed to do.

Note: This is terrifying. Would you want that coming into your room at night? Or at any time? "No" is the answer you are looking for.

Reason Three:

TF sells the collected teeth at the Fairy Market for more than the coinage they leave behind, allowing TF to afford the lavish lifestyle they're used to.

Note: If this turns out to be accurate, I need to start saving my teeth to sell myself because

a) TF is clearly giving me less than they make off the teeth, and

b) my allowance is lacking since my parents started requiring me to finish my chores before getting paid.

Another Note: Find a way to the Fairy Market to sell my teeth myself. And perhaps some homemade jam.

Yet Another Note: Learn to make jam.

Reason Four:

TF is an artist, and their medium (what they use to create their art) is tiny teeth.

> **Note:** You're probably wondering, "Why would TF choose children's teeth for a medium?" My thought: some questions are better left unasked and unanswered, and this seems like one of those questions.

Reason Five:

Here is where I ran into trouble. I had four somewhat decent possibilities, but I wanted a fifth, which I didn't have.

So, I asked my family.

It turned out to be a poor choice.

MY SISTER, ANYA:

Anya didn't answer me because she was video chatting with her friends, even though it was supposed to be mandatory sister time, and demanded I leave her room.

Note: Anya was quite rude. Remember to pay her back in a way that doesn't get me in trouble. Again.

MY MOM: TF keeps them as pets.

Note: Avoid asking Mom for ideas in the future.

MY DAD: To throw at their family when they're annoying.

Note: And Dad.

RALPH: Ralph gave three meows and then ran away. No idea what she was going for.

None of those ideas worked for the final reason, so I decided to go with four!

Looking at my list of possible whys, I wasn't really sold on any of them. There had to be a better one.

Note: Learn to speak cat.

I was now done for the day and decided to try to convince Ralph that she has a future as a

cat model

if she would only let me dress her in my doll clothes.

DAY 3. SATURDAY. 2:45 P.M.

Note: I am aware that Saturday doesn't follow Sunday. I only do investigations on the weekends due to school, soccer, and acting.

Anyway, today was one of my favorite days of the process: Random Thoughts Day!

That's right. To understand where to go next, especially considering that I didn't really like any of my hypotheses from the other day, I needed to write down, without judgment, my every thought about this investigation.

I placed a piece of poster board on the floor and was about to write down all my awesome thoughts.

Note: This used to be done on the wall with no poster board, but after a stern talking-to and an exhausting cleaning of my walls, I no longer write my thoughts on the wall.

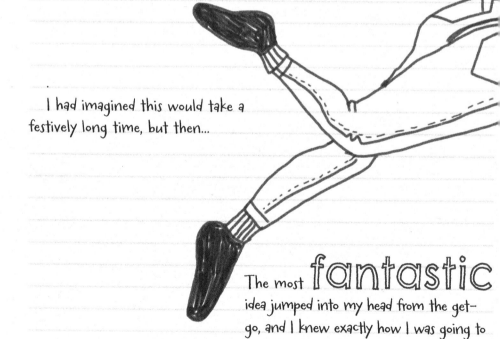

I had imagined this would take a festively long time, but then...

The most fantastic idea jumped into my head from the get-go, and I knew exactly how I was going to find out TF's reason for collecting teeth.

When TF came to collect my tooth, I would

politely tackle TF

and ask sweetly for an answer!

To put this plan into motion, **two** important things must happen:

I must devise a plan for tackling TF in a polite manner.

I must lose a tooth.

Note: I need to research if tackling anyone "politely" is possible and how one goes about asking for something "sweetly."

Another Note: The reason I have to research this whole "asking for something sweetly" is because I've always been quite poor at it. I ask for things rather directly and non-sweetly for a ten-year-old. Or so I've been told. By like every adult.

I did a wiggle check on all my teeth to see if a loss was forthcoming.

Alas, **nothing.**

Since I didn't need to use my poster board for random thoughts, I decided to teach Ralph how to paint.

Note: Teaching Ralph to paint was fun, but I seriously doubt "world-famous artist" is in her future.

Another Note: I can no longer use paint in my room. Parents, am I right?

DAYS 4-10

Still not even a wiggle. Will I ever lose another tooth? Or will I be an adult with a mouth full of baby teeth? And if that happens, what would I look like?

This. I would look like this.

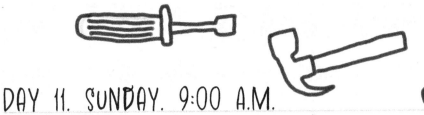

DAY 11. SUNDAY. 9:00 A.M.

ALL my teeth remain in place. I had decided to take out my own tooth using a variety of tools from my tiny toolbox that I keep under my bed, but was stopped several times by my parents. I explained to them that it was for science, but they didn't seem to care.

> **Note:** I am no longer allowed to keep my tiny toolbox in my room.

DAY 12. SATURDAY. 11:30 A.M.

It happened! I lost a tooth, and no, it did not fall off on its own, nor did I yank it out.

How did it happen? I was lying on the floor, pondering how to cure my boredom. I called for Ralph, a known boredom fixer. She came running and, due to her inability to stop quickly, ran directly into my face. Her head collided with my mouth, knocking a tooth out.

> **Note:** Because of her assistance, Ralph was named an honorary assistant and will aid in my capturing of TF.

DAY 13. SUNDAY. 3:30 P.M.

The Plan!

Step One: Sneak Aunt Eunice, our family's body pillow that looks like a body, into my room. Get Ralph to distract everyone.

> **Note:** Ask parents why we have a pillow that looks like a body.

Check! Ralph failed to provide a distraction, but everyone was so into their phones that no one noticed me dragging Aunt Eunice to my room.

> **Note:** File this away for when I become a teenager.

Step Two: Dress Aunt Eunice and make her look like me.

Since she's about twice as tall as me and made of stuffing, I will put my bathrobe on her, make sure the blanket is over her, and hope for the best.

Step Three: Hide Aunt Eunice in my closet until next Saturday, when the plan shall commence.

After my parents tuck me in next
Saturday night, I shall stay awake, reading by the light
of my flashlight until all is quiet. At that moment, I shall switch
places with Aunt Eunice after ensuring my tooth is secure under my pillow.

In the closet, I shall wait until I see TF arrive. As TF is about to make the switch,

booyah!

I jump out, tackle TF politely, and then find out the truth!

Note: I shall not be writing in my journal anytime soon because I will be in deep meditation to prepare for the most important night of my young life.

DAY 14. SUNDAY. 8:00 A.M. OR...
THE DAY AFTER I FOUND OUT THE
Tooth Truth

I now know why TF collects teeth, and tackling wasn't even required. What happened, though, was not what I expected.
Not.   At.   All.

Let me explain. On Saturday night, around 11:36, the house finally grew quiet. I crawled out of bed, grabbed Aunt Eunice from my closet, put my bathrobe on her, placed her in my bed, rechecked my tooth that I had already placed under my pillow, grabbed my flashlight, Ralph (who was asleep on my bed and snoring lightly), and a blanket, and then headed to the closet to wait.

After being in the closet for nothing more than a few minutes and reminding Ralph several times that neither meowing nor scratching at the closet doors were allowed, we both heard a noise and saw a greenish light appear in my room.

Ralph ran to the back of my closet and hid under some clothes I had thrown there when I was forced to clean up the last time. I peeked out and...

There TF was!

Since there are no words that I know that would fully describe what TF looked like, I will use my somewhat decent artistic abilities and draw a picture using the colored pencils I may or may not have taken from Anya's room. Without asking.

Note: I would've asked, but she would have said no, and to do justice to the amazingness of the way TF looked, I needed fancy colored pencils.

I stared in silence for a moment, but my need to complete my plan took over, and I was about to dash out of the closet when TF spoke.

Most Important Note Ever!!!: For this part, I will write it like a story instead of a journal. Format change! It might be a little confusing at first, but you cats are clearly intelligent because you are reading this, so you will adjust. Plus, it's better for the flow! I even throw in a title for free!

A Spirited Non-Journal Retelling of ZEY meeting the TOOTH Fairy

"Hello, Zoey."

I didn't answer. I could only stare while thinking, *TF knows my name.*

"I also know you're hiding in the closet as well. Why don't you and Ralph come out so we can meet each other?"

I slowly opened the closet door and stepped out without Ralph, who was still hiding underneath the dirty clothes that, undoubtedly, would never find their way to my clothes hamper.

TF and I were now standing face-to-face. Well, not actually face-to-face. TF was a smidge taller than I was.

"So, you want to know why I collect teeth?"

"How did you..."

"A tooth fairy knows things." TF smiled.

"Mind reading. I like it."

"One thing I don't understand though, Zoey, is why you didn't simply write me a letter and ask me what you wanted to know."

"Well," I said, "how would I know it was you and not my parents?"

TF nodded. "Good point. But your plan was to tackle me?"

"Politely. And yes, yes it was."

At that moment, Ralph came out of the closet and stood beside me. She looked at TF and meowed. TF laughed.

"I am indeed the Tooth Fairy, Ralph."

My mouth dropped open in shock. "Wait, you speak cat?"

"I speak all creatures. Except squirrels. Now, besides the main question, do you have any other questions you would like to ask me?"

I was so focused on my one question that I hadn't considered any others. So, not wanting to disappoint the Tooth Fairy right at the beginning, I thought up a question as quickly as possible.

"Why under the pillow? Wouldn't it be easier to put the tooth somewhere that wouldn't risk waking the kid up? Plus, it's probably not that sanitary. Kids are gross."

TF laughed.

"Good question, and I have no idea. Perhaps because it's tradition and I'm traditional." TF sat on the edge of my bed. "Now, are you ready to find out why I collect teeth?"

I nodded.

"Wonderful. But how about instead of telling you, I show you. By taking you–"

My eyes grew wide. "To your Tooth Fairy lair? Sweet!"

"I call it my home, but yes. Do you want to come?"

"Absolutely! Should I tell my parents?"

"No need, because for them, you will have never left."

"Time travel. I can dig it."

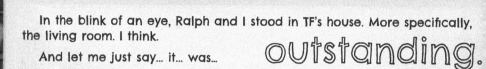

In the blink of an eye, Ralph and I stood in TF's house. More specifically, the living room. I think.

And let me just say... it... was... outstanding.

The ceiling was the night sky on what had to be the starriest night ever. Was it the actual night sky? No idea, but it was definitely not those stick-on glow-in-the-dark stars you put on your ceiling.

Note: Not sure how I feel about furniture that looks like teeth, but I'm not the Tooth Fairy. If I was, I bet I would be all into tooth-shaped furniture.

The walls were what I imagined the inside of a real treehouse looked like, a mix of every color imaginable and some that clearly were only imagined here. Wherever here was.

Note: You may think that so many colors wouldn't work together, but somehow they did. Like all the different colors were always meant to go together to form one tremendously amazing color.

There were lots, and I mean lots, of portraits on the wall of what I believed to be other tooth fairies. Were they tooth fairies of long ago, or were there multiple tooth fairies flying about collecting teeth at the same time? Or were they tooth fairies at all? Maybe they were TF's family. Or total strangers.

Note: I don't know why TF would have pictures of strangers hanging on the wall, but I couldn't eliminate the possibility until I knew for sure.

Another Note: I suppose I will never know for sure because I forgot to ask. My apologies, but as you read on, you'll understand why.

There were tiny trinkets everywhere, which I imagine TF picked up from their travels around the world.

Note: By "picked up," I don't mean to imply "stole." I simply mean that TF probably took time to do a little souvenir shopping.

There was so much to see that I totally forgot why I had come in the first place.

"You're standing with your mouth open, Zoey."

I shut my mouth and turned to TF. "Your house is amazing. Like everything in it."

"And to think, you haven't seen everything. In fact, the most amazing part of the house is right in front of you, yet it remains unseen."

I was confused. I looked at Ralph, and even though I find Ralph to be a highly rated cat overall, TF couldn't have been talking about her. But the only other thing was a table with a tiny box on it. TF couldn't mean that

"I do."

"But it's just a wooden table with a box on it. I mean, compared to the rest of your house..."

"The rest of the house cannot compare to that *tiny box.*"

"I don't understand."

"You see, Zoey, this is where every tooth I collect goes." TF took something out of a little bag attached to their robe, then looked at me. "Your *tooth.*"

The box on the table opened on its own, and my tooth flew into it like it knew where it belonged. The lid then slowly closed. "No matter how many teeth I collect, there's always enough room for one more," TF said.

"How?" I asked. "Wait. Magic, right?"

"That's right. And I leave a small token, or as you say, 'coinage,' behind for each child because what's inside of the teeth is quite valuable."

"Really? There's a market for pulp, dentin, enamel, and cementum?"

"Not sure, but I love that you know what a tooth is made of. But there *is* something special in every child's tooth."

"What?"

"Why, the most important aspect of childhood: Wonder."

"It's why children like you can see all the colors of the world and all the possibilities that life possesses. Yet, as people get older, they often lose that wonder."

"What happens when they lose wonder?"

"The world becomes gray, less beautiful. Then hope and joy fade."

"That's super sad. But how does a tiny tooth fix that?"

TF pointed to the box. "When the tooth is placed here, it ceases being what it was."

"So, it's no longer a tooth?"

"No, it becomes the essence of childhood."

"Wonder."

TF nodded. "That's right. Then, when teens and adults are in their darkest times, when all possibility and hope are gone, the box opens and releases that wonder. It finds its way to the one in need, and for a moment, hope is restored."

"But why only a moment? Won't they get sad again?"

"Of course, but sometimes it only takes one moment of wonder to create a spark and restore hope. When hope is restored, amazing things can happen."

"Cool."

Out of nowhere, TF's house began to shake. Like really shake. I looked for Ralph, but she had already jumped into TF's arms.

Note: I will mention this betrayal in our meeting next month.

I grabbed onto the tooth-shaped couch and looked at TF. "Is this an earthquake? I'm pretty knowledgeable about earthquakes because I've read like 3½ books about them, and this feels like what I read about."

"Don't be afraid, Zoey. It's not an earthquake. Look."

TF pointed to the tiny box, which was shaking more violently than the house. Emerald-green lights started shooting from it.

"There's much need today."
"You mean…"

"I do." TF extended their hand to me, and I took it. "Let me show you how it works."

And for the second time, Ralph and I found ourselves flying.

Then we saw the most incredible and beautiful things ever. I will do my best to recreate them, but it's going to be super difficult because everything I saw... totally life-changing.

Suddenly, we were all back in my room.

"That was the most spectacular thing I have ever seen in my life, and I've seen a lot. I am ten, after all."

TF smiled. "Now you know why I do what I do."

"I do. Thank you."

"You are very welcome. Perhaps you could share what you've learned? Maybe write a book about it?"

"That's a fantastic idea! I've always wanted to write a book!"

"I know, and it's going to be wonderful."

"Thanks, but I'll be happy with 'perfectly adequate.'"

"Of course."

TF turned and started heading to the window. "Well, I must be on my way. Much more collecting to do tonight." TF looked back at me. "It was delightful meeting you and Ralph, Zoey."

"You, too." I then realized something. "Wait, am I going to see how you get out of rooms?"

"That, my dear, is a trade secret."

"But I feel like..."

DAY 15. MONDAY. BEFORE LEAVING FOR SCHOOL.

   I never finished that statement because the next thing I knew, it was morning, and I was waking up with Ralph sleeping on my head. I sat up quickly and looked at her. "Was it a dream, Ralph?"

   Ralph meowed, but since I still don't know how to speak cat, I had no idea if she said yes or no.

   But then I remembered. I reached underneath my pillow and felt what I imagined to be an envelope. It was. A very stylish green one. I opened it and discovered coinage and a note, which I would share now, but I'm going to save it for the dramatic conclusion of the story.

DAY 16. SATURDAY.
THE END OF THE STORY.

Well, this brings my Tooth Fairy investigation to a close.

Everything you read here happened just the way I said it did, except for the things I couldn't remember and had to make up.

Before ending this type of story, research on how to end a book in an amazing way has told me that I must do two things.

The Two Things

Set up a possible sequel.

Say something heartfelt to the readers to pack an emotional wallop, whatever that means.

First, let's set up the sequel, or my next investigation, which I already have an idea for. Looking at you,

Easter Bunny.

Such a focus on eggs when bunnies give birth to live young. What's that about, EB? Not that I think hiding baby bunnies is a wise idea, even though searching for them would be so fun and cute. Though I would not call it a "Baby Bunny Hunt" because that sounds disturbing.

Note: I don't really have a lot for the Easter Bunny investigation yet. And if you expected more from me, you need to R - E - L - A - X. I just solved the why of the Tooth Fairy, and I'm tired. Plus, I really want to play.

And finally, the emotional wallop part.

Besides leaving coinage, TF also wrote me something which I will share now. I figure it's the best possible way to end this story. By the way, TF's handwriting is outstanding. Very whimsical. And that's how we end! Keep on wondering, peeps!

Zoey out!

Dear Zoey,

I'm so glad that you tried to capture me. You are delightfully charming, and I'm quite the fan. Always remember that the world is a lovely place, even when it seems like it's not, with wonder often hidden right in front of you or just around the corner. Always be on the lookout for it, for when you find it, you will also find beauty, hope, and possibility. Trust me on this. And if there ever comes a time when you can't find it, I'll make sure it finds you.

Love,

TF

Note: TF wasn't just talking to me. That message, dear readers, was meant for all of us.

CPSIA information can be obtained
at www.ICGtesting.com
Printed in the USA
BVHW011731160223
658686BV00019B/339